The Doctor's Secret

For my family who have been forced to listen to me talk about Tom Dooley for 18 years and especially for my son Tim who has faithfully followed me on many of my journeys to the places where the events took place.

Thank you to all the people from Caldwell, Iredell and Wilkes counties in Western North Carolina who have helped and inspired me along the way.

A special thank you to Charlotte and Bill Barnes who introduced me to almost everyone else and to Margaret Carter Martine and Sharon Carter Underwood for letting me use their mother's painting as the cover illustration.

Jan Kronsell

THE DOCTOR'S SECRET

Another version of the Tom Dooley legend

Cover illustration:
Copy of a painting by Edith Marie Ferguson Carter (1930 – 2014).
Courtesy of Whippoorwill Academy and Village, Ferguson, North Carolina.

Published by: Books on Demand GmbH, Copenhagen, Denmark
Printed by: Books on Demand GmbH, Norderstedt, Germany

ISBN: 978-87-7188-248-3

Author's Foreword

On May 1st 1868 Thomas C. Dula (later known to the world as Tom Dooley) was hanged on Depot Hill on the southern outskirts of Statesville in Iredell County, North Carolina for the murder of his girlfriend, Laura Foster in neighboring Wilkes County almost two years earlier.

All through the trial and even standing at the gallows Tom Dooley claimed his innocence and swore that hadn't some of the witnesses committed perjury, he wouldn't have been convicted.

Soon after the execution and maybe even before that, rumors spread in the community where the murder had taken place that Tom did not kill Laura Foster, and that the real killer was his jealous, married lover, Ann Melton, in some stories assisted by her maid, Pauline Foster, and that Tom only helped to bury the body because he loved Ann. Over time these rumors developed into several different legends and when the case was made famous by the Kingston Trio's hit in 1958, The Ballad of Tom Dooley, which had been recorded several times before, these legends had a revival and became popular again and they live on to this day.

One persistent legend tells, that before her death, Ann Melton told the physician, who treated her *"something that would have saved Tom from the gallows"*. This novella is partially based on this legend. It also includes material from several other legends including one, that I have only heard once, and which may have been invented by the man who told it to me, as I have never heard or read about it elsewhere, but as it fitted well into my story, I used it anyway.

I have put the prologue and epilogue in the mouth of a fictional, modern day lawyer from Raleigh, but all the other people mentioned in the novella are historical characters, and except from the plot and my suggested solution to the riddle, everything else, like the family relationships between the involved, what was said at the trial and so on can be verified by the few existing trial records, historic census records, marriage licenses, birth and death certificates and other public records together with contemporary newspaper articles, and other public and private records.

Most of the people I mention in this book still have living descendants, and I have spoken to a few of them. My intention is not to insult their ancestors, but only to tell a tale, a tale about how it could have happened.

So please read this novella as a piece of fiction, not as a history book.

Brøndby, Denmark, December 2018
Jan Kronsell

Publisher's prologue:

My name is Matthew Murphy and I'm a lawyer in Raleigh, North Carolina. I work for C. A. Murphy and Associates, Attorneys at Law. The firm was founded by my great-great-grandfather in 1910, and ever since that, the family has produced at least one lawyer in each generation. My great-great-grandfather, my great-grandfather and my grandfather have all gone to a better place, unless the old saying is true, that the Devil takes all lawyers. Today I'm running the firm together with four other lawyers and an office staff of 10. About one year ago, we were notified, that the building, that had housed our offices since my great-great-grandfather expanded from an office in his own home in 1920, was to be torn down to give room for a residential building to create housing space for Raleigh's ever growing population. We therefore had to look for new accommodations, which actually came at the right time, as business has been growing a lot lately, and we may have to employ more people soon.

We found a new place in a modern office building, not far from the old place, and rented a larger office, where there is room for further expansion. So about one month ago, we started to pack everything in boxes in order to be ready for our move. One afternoon my secretary entered my office, carrying a thick, brown and dusty envelope in her hand. She told me, she had discovered this envelope behind a filing cabinet, and that it looked as if it had been there for years, and that I'd better take a look at it. On the front of the envelope was only a few words written in a handwriting, that I recognized as my great-great-grandfather's from all the old documents that my father had forced me to read, when I first started in the firm. The writing only said: "Do not open this envelope until 1989 at the earliest." This sounded strange as we are now in 2018, so I called my father who has retired but is still very much alive and kicking and as sharp as always, but he knew nothing about the envelope and had neither seen it, nor heard of it at least as far as he remembered, so it must have been hidden behind the filing cabinet for 50 years or more, as my father started in the firm in 1967.

I decided to open the envelope, and inside I found another thick and rather strange looking rhombus shaped envelope that was apparently home-made, and seemed to be very old. It was closed with strings and sealed in four places with wax seals. Along with the envelope was a rather long letter, also handwritten. I will not go through the letter, as it contained a lot of things that had nothing to do with the envelope, but it was certain that the sender of the letter had been a close friend of my great-great-grandfather. Near the end of the letter was a passage that mentioned the envelope though:

"Sometime in 1888, I received the enclosed envelope from my father. He made me swear that I would make sure that it would not be opened until one hundred years after his death. In 1889 my father passed away and I have kept the letter until now. I hope that you, my dear friend and attorney, will relieve me of the responsibility, as I fear that I have not very much time left myself, and I will not let my children in on this strange matter. I know that you, as my lawyer, will do as requested and as a friend I trust you to do so."

There was a bit more in the letter, and it was signed

Kings Creek, North Carolina, January 12th, 1925.
Your friend
George Hill Carter

As I was rather busy at the time, and almost 30 years had passed since the letter was supposed to have been opened, I postponed it to a later time as I didn't think that a few more days would matter. I brought the envelope back home with me that night, but I didn't get to open it, until the following weekend. Before opening the envelope, I had done a bit of research and discovered that Kings Creek was a small populated place in Caldwell County in the western part of the state, and that there had actually at one time lived a George Hill Carter in that area, a physician who had died back in 1926, so I guessed that this was the man, who had sent the letter to my great-great-grandfather.

When I finally opened the envelope I found a large bundle of papers tied together with a string. They were all written in a handwriting that was rather hard to read and sometimes I had to use a magnifying glass, and even sometimes had to guess, but the manuscript was clearly written by an educated man. The manuscript told a story that I had actually been aware of but didn't know much about, and when I later researched it, I discovered, that what was in the manuscript did appear in many versions of the story, except for the most essential and personal parts, that only the author and a few others would know.

As per the author's request I have therefore decided to publish this manuscript. If what it contains is correct, one man will finally get justice as it was clear from the manuscript that he had been treated unjustly. But I will let the author tell his story even if I had made some changes in order to modernize the language just a little bit and corrected the spelling where the original spelling was different from how we spell today. I have added some punctuation of which there was almost none and a few line breaks here and there. Finally, I have divided the long manuscript into a few chapters. These chapters and their headings are all my inventions. I have added a few comments along the way just to clarify some things, that probably is not known today. These comments are typed in the same font as this prologue and placed in square brackets.

The Background

I write this to clear something of my mind that has been weighing heavily on my conscience for almost 15 years. When I first learned what I am about to tell you, I had to swear never to tell anybody for as long as I lived though, and that promise I have kept, even if it has been very hard for me. But now I will try to clear my conscience before I die as I fear I have not long time left to live. I will give this letter to my son in a closed and sealed envelope and make him swear that he and his descendants will not open it until at least one hundred years after my passing. The story I am about to tell has probably long been forgotten when this letter is finally opened. At least I hope it is, and anyone involved in the matter will be long gone like me. I have to tell my story though as a great injustice was done. Even if the man, suffering from this injustice has already been dead for almost 20 years, I hope that his immortal soul and maybe mine as well, if such a thing exists, will be redeemed, when the truth is finally revealed. But let me begin with telling you, what the background for my confession actually was – if you could call this a confession, as I actually do not confess anything myself, except for a guilty conscience.

My name is George Nicholas Carter. I was born and raised in Shelton, Virginia, but at the age of 27, after having completed my medical studies, I moved from my home in Virginia to North Carolina, more specifically to a small town called Hamptonville. Here I joined forces with another physician that I had met at the medical school. His name was Abel Cowles, and we both stayed in the home of his father, Josiah Cowles, a very wealthy plantation owner and politician. Once while I was there, Abel's older brother, Calvin, who owned a general store in the small settlement, Elkville in western Wilkes County, came for a visit. Together with him was another landowner from the area known as Happy Valley, where Calvin had established his store. This man was Catlett Jones who was later to become my father-in-law. Calvin Cowles invited me and his brother to visit him in Elkville which we did, some months later. While there I met the youngest daughter of Catlett Jones, Juliet, and I fell hopelessly in love with her.

Fortunately, she returned my love, and in 1851, I moved to the area, settling on land, that I bought from one of Catlett Jones' neighbors. In 1852 I married Juliet, and I have stayed in Kings Creek ever since, and they will bury me here, next to Juliet, when my time is up. But let me get back to my story; and excuse an old man for letting his mind and memories lead him astray from time to time.

Twenty-one years ago a young girl by the name of Laura Foster disappeared from my neighborhood in Yadkin Valley in the western part of North Carolina never to be seen alive again. Laura Foster had for some time been a patient of mine as she was suffering from the terrible disease known locally as "the pox", but better known in the medical world as syphilis. Unfortunately, many others in both my local area and elsewhere suffered from this disease before, under and after the terrible Civ il War, and the disease is still plaguing our nation. A young man, Thomas C. Dula, another patient of mine, also suffering from syphilis, was arrested and accused of having murdered her. Several months later the dead body was found in a shallow grave by my friend and neighbor, Colonel James Isbell and his father-in-law, Major David E. Horton. Thomas Dula was finally put to trial after having been in jail for almost two months, even if nobody knew whether a crime had even been committed or if Laura Foster had just eloped. On trial with him was yet another patient of mine, Ann Melton, who was accused of being his accomplice.

As I mentioned earlier, the story that I'm about to tell will probably and hopefully long be forgotten when this letter is read, so I will give you a little more background, just to let you know what actually happened near the county line between Wilkes and Caldwell counties in North Carolina in the spring of 1866, two years after the end of the war between the nations. Most of what I tell you here I learned during the trials, even if I knew some from previous contacts with the people involved. I was after all their physician, and the only one in a large area, so little by little I got to know most of the people from the hills as well as the people from the valley.

Thomas Dula, the man who was eventually convicted and hanged for the murder, was the youngest of seven siblings, three sons and four daughters, born to Mary and Thomas P. Dula. His grandfather, Bennett Dula was one of the first Dulas to arrive in Happy Valley only about a year and a half after his sister Judith, who had moved to the valley, when she married Thomas Hall. Between Judith and Bennett, another brother, William, known as Captain Dula had settled in the valley. Both Judith and the two brothers had passed away long before I arrived in the valley though. To the best of my knowledge, Captain Dula, my wife's maternal grandfather, passed away in 1835 while Thomas Dula's grandfather had passed away back in 1822, the same year I was born and that Thomas P, and Mary Dula were married. This I learned from Mary Dula, while I was looking after her husband when he was ill. I do not know when Judith Dula Hall passed away, but she was the grandmother of Rufus Dula Hall, an important witness at the trial and Thomas Dula's second cousin. She was also the great-grandmother of Louisa Gilbert, whom James Melton married after Ann Melton's tragic death; thus Thomas Dula and Louisa Gilbert were second cousins once removed. I am sorry if I digress from the story here and there, but every time I think back, I cannot help wondering how everyone connected to the case was related to one another.

Thomas Dula's father passed away in 1854, a few years after my arrival in the valley, when Thomas was only nine years old. Not that I had anything to do with his death. He died during one of the many flu epidemics that haunted the land and there was nothing I could do to save him, and even if a lot of people survived these epidemics, many were not so lucky. At the time of the murder Thomas Dula lived with his mother and his older sister in a cabin in the hills north of the river, on land that she had inherited from her husband. Until his death the family had lived in the valley south of the river in the house that Bennett Dula had built, when he arrived in the valley. When the older Thomas Dula passed away, the family home was overtaken by his younger brother, called Bennett after his father. Bennett Dula still lives in the house with his wife and children.

Thomas Dula had been a soldier during the terrible civil war and had been taken prisoner and send to a prison camp in Maryland, but survived and returned to Elkville when the war was over. Neither of his two older brothers survived the war though and he was thus the only son left to help his mother run the farm. Long before the war, when he was only about 14 years of age and she was 15, Thomas Dula engaged in a carnal relationship, with a neighbor girl, Ann Foster, and this relationship continued even after Ann was married to James Melton in 1859, and did not end until Thomas joined the army in March of 1862 together with his older brother, William. James Melton had already joined the army in April 1861 as he was about six years older than Thomas Dula. Mr. Dula was a little over 20 years when he returned from the war, having lied himself older in order to be recruited. Of course he was not the only one that returned. So did a lot of other young men, like Thomas Dula's best friend, George Washington Anderson, and James Melton, Ann Melton's husband who had been imprisoned in the same prison camp as Thomas Dula.

After the war Ann Melton and Thomas Dula had taken up their illicit relationship once again, I know because Thomas Dula told me so himself, when he came to get treatment for his disease and it was also mentioned during the trials. Ann Melton was not the only woman Thomas Dula courted; actually he was what people back in Virginia might call a philanderer. [Publisher's note: A philanderer is and old expression for what we today would probably call a womanizer.] He liked the ladies and apparently many liked him back, and not just the unmarried women, some of the married as well, like Ann Melton. The local rumors named at least two or three married women, but these rumors did not arise until after the execution, when Thomas Dula could neither deny nor confirm these illicit relationships, and even if names were mentioned at the time, I will not do so as most were only unconfirmed rumors. In court it was revealed that he had relationships with some unmarried women as well and three names were mentioned.

One of these unmarried women was Laura Foster, the girl that was killed. She lived in German Hill in Caldwell County, in the hills, less than three miles from my farm, with her father and two younger siblings. Her mother and two other siblings had died from another flu epidemic, this one in 1864 while the war was still going on. Her father, Wilson Foster, had once owned a good tract of land, but lost it to bad circumstances before the war, and now worked as a sharecropper and farm laborer on different farms, and so did her younger brother, James, while the youngest, Elbert, was at home, doing chores around their own cabin. Wilson Foster was the proud owner of a horse though, but he had no stable, so normally he just tied the horse to a tree outside the cabin. This was the horse that Laura took the Friday morning she disappeared; the horse that had returned to the Foster home the very next morning. This I already knew before the trial, as I was the family's physician during their illness, but like it was the case with Thomas Dula's father ten years before, there was nothing I could do, when Mary Foster and her children was ill with the flu, even if I did my best, but there was and still is no remedy for this disease, at least none of those I tried helped the poor mother and her children, and I know of none that will.

Another unmarried woman that Thomas Dula courted, was Pauline Foster (or Purlene as she was called in the local dialect, that also pronounces Laura as Laurie and Anna as Anny). She was a distant cousin of Ann Melton as well as of Laura Foster, and she was an illegitimate first cousin once removed of Thomas Dula as her father was Dula's first cousin. Levi Foster, Pauline's father, was an illegitimate son of Thomas' uncle, Jack Dula. Of course also Ann Melton and Laura Foster were distantly related to one another. Actually most of the people in Happy Valley and the surrounding hills, were and still are related to each other, either by blood or by marriage. At the time of the murder Pauline Foster worked as a farm laborer with Ann Melton and her husband, James, in order to earn money for her syphilis treatment.

The last of the three unmarried women named in court was one Caroline Barnes. She was the 18-year-old daughter of a wealthy farmer, Manly Barnes, who had his home in the valley, not far from the Foster home in the hills. Mr. Barnes definitely did not like Thomas Dula, who he was sure had seduced his daughter in order to get at his wealth, though I am not so sure who seduced whom. Caroline Barnes, even if only 18 at the time, was the kind of person, who if she wanted something, would not give up until she got what she wanted. But I knew that Dula always tried to avoid meeting Mr. Barnes if he could.

From what I understood from the testimonies, Thomas Dula and Laura Foster knew each other before the war but only as people in the area generally knew each other. When he was released from the prison camp, and returned to Elkville, he met her at the store a couple of times, and started wooing her, and in early January 1866 they became lovers. Not that this relationship prevented any of them from seeing other people as well. The relationship only lasted a couple of months though, then they stopped seeing each other around the beginning of March. From testimonies in court, I learned that Thomas Dula had visited her again a couple of times near the end of May and right before she disappeared. I guess that these visits, after two months, may have caused the prosecution to believe, that Dula was the culprit. At least it caused me to believe so, when I found out.

After Laura Foster's disappearance, but before the body was found, in late June, Thomas Dula left the area. At that time three people were arrested in connection with the murder, but was let go again as no evidence pointed in their direction. These people were Ann Melton and then two of Thomas Dula's first cousins, Ann Pauline Dula and Granville Dula, both children of his uncle, the younger Bennett Dula. I never found out why the latter two was put under arrest in the first place, but either Wilson Foster who asked the justice of peace to have them arrested, must have thought that they had something to do with Laura's disappearance, or the justice of peace may have misunderstood whom Wilson wanted arrested and put them on the arrest warrant by mistake. Later Pauline Foster was also arrested, as I explained in my testimony in court, but she too was let go.

Sheriff Hix of Wilkes County swore in two deputy sheriffs, Ben Ferguson and John Adkins, both from Elkville, who knew Thomas Dula, and they were send to bring him back, as he was rumored to have left for Tennessee. About two weeks after his leaving the area, they did bring him home with the help of one Tennessee colonel, James Grayson, who had also helped capture him. They brought him to Wilkesboro and delivered him to Sheriff Hix, who incarcerated him in the new jail there.

In late August the body had still not been discovered, but Pauline Foster, who in several drunken stupors had bragged about knowing something about or even taking part in the murder, was arrested once again. In court she later testified that she had only said what she did in jest. But she told the sheriff that she knew where the body was buried, because Ann Melton had shown her the grave, and she promised that if she was set free, she would show them. She was then brought back to Elkville, where a search party was organized, and she showed the party part of the way. She then pointed in a direction up the hill side, and said that she knew the body was buried up there somewhere, but she did not know exactly where, as the place they had reached at that time, was as far as she had gone with Ann Melton. The search party split up in pairs and started searching the hill side. My neighbor, James Isbell, paired off with his father-in-law, Major David Horton, and when the major's horse snorted in a thicket of laurels, they found the grave. They summoned the rest of the search party, and removed the dirt. In the grave they found the body of a woman, and then they sent for me. When I arrived I examined the body as best as I could which was not that good. But I noticed that the grave was so short that her knees had been bent in order for the body to fit. The body was removed from the shallow and too short grave and carried to Cowles' Store where I examined it more thoroughly. I found a single stab wound in the chest, but the body was so disintegrated, that I could not determine, if the knife had hit the heart or not. The body was carried to her home, and as Wilson Foster did not own any land, she found her final resting place the very same day on a plot of land belonging to one of her father's neighbors, John Walter Winkler, a farmer that Wilson Foster had done farm work for. Pauline Foster was let go as she had been promised, and instead Ann Melton was arrested and incarcerated in Wilkes County Jail next to Thomas Dula.

As the murder of Laura Foster took place in Wilkes County, the trial opened in Wilkesboro, but was soon transferred to Statesville in Iredell County by request of the defendants and their lawyer, the former North Carolina governor, Zebulon Vance, who is at present representing North Carolina in the US Senate. As I had examined the body of Laura Foster, when it was found, I was called to testify, together with many other witnesses from our community. I was present during all the days in court, but I will not bother you with all that happened, and what everybody said. Pauline Foster was the key witness for the prosecution, but in my opinion her testimony did not actually do much harm to Thomas Dula, as the only one she was really incriminating was actually her employer and relative, Ann Melton. A lot of other witnesses was heard, but none of them actually knew anything about the murder, and most of the testimonies were about Thomas Dula's whereabouts before and after Laura Foster disappeared. I am not a lawyer, but in my opinion many of the testimonies were rather irrelevant. I will just give you one example like one witness who testified that she had seen Thomas Dula on the road, three miles from Laura Foster's home two days before Laura disappeared. That was actually only about one mile from my home and he did come to visit me for treatment early that Wednesday. How his being on the road far away from Laura's home two days before her disappearance could have any significance, I still wonder. Especially because we had already heard from Wilson Foster's testimony, that Thomas Dula did visit Laura Foster that Wednesday.

The witness who in my opinion did most damage to Dula's case, was a mulatto woman, Elizabeth Scott, who was a neighbor of the Fosters. She claimed that she had met Laura Foster on that faithful morning, and that Laura had told her, that she was going to meet Dula. I believe that it was this testimony more than anything else that turned the jury against Thomas Dula as it made most people, and probably also the jury, believe that the two of them were actually going to meet that morning. And it convinced me as well. And now, this many years later, when I know the truth of what really happened, I have to admit, that Mr. Caldwell, the prosecutor, was very good at making everyday things that Thomas Dula and Ann Melton did before and after Laura's disappearance look suspicious, but I also have to admit, that I never thought about it that way at the time of the trials though.

When the jury returned with a guilty verdict, Mr. Vance asked for an appeal to the supreme court because he thought that hearsay had been allowed and he especially mentioned the testimony from Elizabeth Scott about what Laura Foster had told her. The appeal was granted by the presiding judge, The Honorable Ralph Buxton, and the case was sent to the supreme court. This I only learned at a later time from my friend, John Clement, who was a member of the prosecution team as at that time I had returned home from Statesville, to be with my family and take care of my patients. The supreme court ordered a new trial, and in the spring term of 1867 I was once more called as a witness, and had to go to Statesville, only to be sent home again, as Mr. Vance presented an affidavit claiming that the two people accused of the crime could not have a fair trial, as three defense witnesses were absent. On the grounds of this affidavit, the presiding judge, Mr. Gelliam, postponed the trial to the fall term of 1867, and we could all return to our homes. In October we went to Statesville once more and this time the prosecutor asked for a postponement as three of his witnesses were now absent. The presiding judge, Mr. Little, could do nothing else than postpone the trial once more until the spring term of 1868.

But the governor of that time, Mr. Jonathan Worth, had apparently gotten tired of all these postponements, and there was also a lot of other serious cases waiting for trial in Statesville, so the governor ordered the honorable William Shipp, one of the best judges in the state, or at least so my lawyer acquaintances say, to set up a Court of Oyer and Terminer, to close all these cases. [Publisher's note: A Court of Oyer and Terminer was a special court that only had jurisdiction over serious crimes, punishable by life imprisonment or death. In the times after the Civil War, courts of oyer and terminer handled criminal cases against slaves and other defendants that had been disenfranchised, though Tom Dooley's rights had not been disenfranchised in any way. Such a court could be established by order of the governor like in this case, but as far as I have been able to discover it has only been used a very few times in North Carolina.] So in January we went back to Statesville for what proved to be the final trial. Once again the jury found Thomas Dula guilty, and once again he was allowed an appeal, but this time the Supreme court found that no errors had been made, so the verdict was not changed. All through his incarceration and trial Thomas Dula had claimed his innocence, but not many believed him, not even me at that time.

On the First of May 1868 Thomas Dula was hanged in Statesville and even at the gallows he swore his innocence and claimed that some of the witnesses had sworn falsely against him. I, as well as many others from the communities of Kings Creek, German Hill and Elkville, where Laura Foster, Thomas Dula and Ann Melton had lived, and who all had been witnesses at the trial, were present at the execution. I later read in a newspaper, that more than 3.000 people had been present, most from out of town as the population in Statesville only numbered around 600 inhabitants at the time. To me and many other people as well it was surprising how many of the bystanders were women and even children.

The newspaper article

At the end of May 1868, about one month after the execution had taken place, I received a letter from a good friend from medical school, with whom I have maintained contact to this day. He is a physician in New York City, and we write letters to each other three or four times a year and I have even visited him there a couple of times like he has visited me. Our exchange of letters, of course, had been impossible during the years when our states were enemies in the terrible war. Not because our friendship had diminished; it was just not possible to send mail as usual as he had enrolled as a physician in the Union Army. Some months after the end of the war, in the fall of 1865 I wrote him a letter and he responded, and we soon returned to the same rate of exchanging letters as before the war. The letter I am talking about arrived in mid July 1868, and it was nothing special, just one of his usual letters, talking about this and that, but in the letter he had enclosed a clipping from a New York newspaper, the New York Herald from May 2nd, the day after Thomas Dula was hanged in Statesville. The newspaper had apparently had a reporter present at the execution, and he had written about the case as well as the aforementioned terrible event that had put a man to his death.

However, it was difficult to recognize the description the journalist gave in his report. Much of it seemed uncertain and some was very much exaggerated while other things were completely false and made up. I am not going to oppose all of his claims here, but, among other things, he wrote that Laura Foster was pregnant when she was murdered. It was certainly not the case, which I should know as she was my patient, and it was I who examined her dead body when it was found, and even if the body was rather decomposed, there was no sign of any pregnancy. However, it was true when the journalist wrote that Thomas Dula made a long speech at the gallows, and it is also true that in this speech he accused several people, including my neighbor and friend, James Isbell, of lying in court. It was also alleged in the article that Thomas Dula had written not only a confession but also a long description of his life on his last night in the cell before his execution. But I am sure that this was untrue. Two years earlier, when he was my patient, he could only write his own name and a few short sentences with great difficulty and with my help. Later the very short confession was used when the case against Ann Melton came to trial, but as far as I know, and I have asked a lot of people from Statesville, no-one but the journalist has ever seen the 15-page story of his life that the newspaper referred to. But the biggest mistake the reporter made was in his description of the area in which we live.

"The community in the vicinity of this tragedy is divided into two entirely separate and distinct classes. The one occupying the fertile lands adjacent to the Yadkin river and its tributaries is educated and intelligent, and the other, living on the spurs and ridges of the mountains, is ignorant, poor and depraved. A state of morality unexampled in the history of any country exists among these people, and such a general system of free-loveism prevails that it is "a wise child that knows its father." This is the Bates Place, where the body was discovered by blood marks, and where some ten or twelve families are living in the manner described. It is a poor country, covered with thickets and a dense undergrowth, and an attempt had been made to conceal the blood by covering it with bushes."

These were the words of the journalist, as they could be read in the newspaper. I still have the clipping in my possession to this day.

When I arrived in Caldwell County in 1851 before my wedding to my dear wife Juliet, who unfortunately passed away 5 years ago, only 55 years old, I discovered that a few, very large families owned most of the land in Happy Valley. Those were the Joneses (my wife's family), the Hortons, the Isbells, the Witherspoons, the Fergusons and the Dulas. There were of course other families but these were the most important and to a large extend almost any other family in the area was married into one of these families. And the important families were of course married into one another as well. As an example I can mention that my neighbor and friend, James Isbell was thus married to Sarah Louise Horton and his sister Martha Louisa was married to Sarah's brother, Larkin Horton while another sister, Mildred Horton was married to my wife's youngest brother, Charles. And as there were many marriages where two or more siblings from one family married two or more siblings from another family, double cousins were abundant in the area. Also marriages between cousins and even uncles and nieces and aunts and nephews were not rare because of the large age differences between siblings, which meant that a man could very well be older than his aunt or a women older than her uncle.

But what surprised me most, yes I dare say almost shocked me, when I first arrived in Happy Valley, was the many children in the area that were born out of wedlock. So in this matter the journalist was right. Free love was practiced in the area, but definitely not only among the poor people of the hills; it happened equally among the wealthier people living in the valley. And it was not only the unmarried women who had illegitimate children. There were also many married couples where husbands had children with women other than their wives, and married women had children with other men than their husbands! Neither is it true that the two classes lived completely separate lives and never got together. How could they have avoided that?

First of all, they worked together as many of the less wealthy worked on the farms of the wealthier and more fortunate, and they also met at the local store when political meetings were held there, when trials for the local justice of the peace took place or they simply went there to shop. Even if my friend Calvin Cowles had sold his general store to Phineas Horton way back in 1858 and moved to Wilkesboro with his wife, Martha, he still owned land in our area, now grown by a tenant, and from old habit the store was still known as Cowles' Store. Later Calvin Cowles, who was a Republican became president of the constitutional congress in Raleigh in 1868 that gave us a new constitution, which led to a quarrel with his younger half-brother, Andrew, who was a Democrat, and the two of them never have reconciled to the best of my knowledge. Calvin's first wife, Martha died in April 1866, and in 1868, a couple of months after the execution of Thomas Dula, he married Ida Holden, daughter of governor William Holden and more than 25 years younger than he was. I was invited to the wedding with my wife as he had been invited and taken part in mine together with his first wife, but I had to go alone as Juliet was not feeling well enough to travel to Raleigh where the wedding took place. But I digress here and I must get back to my story.

When people from both the valley and hills met for work or shopping they socialized with each other no matter what class they belonged to, even if it is true that most socializing was due to them either working together or meeting coincidentally more than having a really social relationship. The lower classes were seldom invited to dances held by the wealthy people (even if it happened from time to time) and vice versa even if Thomas Dula, before his arrest, sometimes played at our dances, together with his wealthy second cousin, Rufus Dula Horton. Both were terrific fiddle players.

It was necessary to help each other in the hard times after the unfortunate war between the states, and everybody had to stick together to survive. Finally, many of the poor were and still is closely related to the wealthier. Thomas Dula was thus my wife's second cousin, and he was also a second cousin of my neighbor, James Isbell's wife. By the way, Bates Place was not an area, as the journalist wrote in his article, but the name of a particular place where once a blacksmith's shop had been and nobody lived there at that time. Should the area where the unfortunate events took place actually have been given a name, it would rather be "Reedy Branch", named for the small creek that runs through the area towards the Yadkin River, as most of the homes in the area are located close to this creek. And the body was not found at Bates Place but on a ridge between three quarters of a mile and one mile from Bates Place, in the direction of where Mary Dula had her home. And no blood marks led to the discovery of the grave, as Laura Foster was killed elsewhere, and it was the fact that Major Horton's horse snorted at the place that turned his and James Isbell's attention to the fact that the earth has been dug up and replaced.

One of the things that the newspaper article claims, is completely false, and either a very hateful and malicious person have told the reporter this, or the journalist may have invented the story all by himself to show how depraved the people in the area were, thus creating a scandal, and I later found out that this newspaper was known for doing things like that just to sell more copies of the paper.

"Pauline Foster, the principal witness against both the accused, is remarkable for nothing but debasement, and may be dismissed with the statement that she has since married a white man and given birth to a negro child...."

As I mentioned earlier, Pauline Foster was a distant cousin of Ann Melton and of Laura Foster too, as her maternal grandmother was a paternal great-aunt of both of them. Actually most of the people in Happy Valley and the surrounding hills, were and still are related to each other, either by blood or by marriage.

While it is true that Pauline was not exactly one of God's angels, she did not indulge herself in any more depravity than did so many others. And that she should have gotten a negro child is simply untrue. She actually married John Scott, at the end of 1867, about a year after the first trial, and she did give birth to a son in March 1868 after the second trial and before Thomas Dula was hanged, but as I saw the baby only a few weeks after it was born when I visited Watauga County to call on a colleague there, I could say with complete certainty that this child was not a negro or mulatto but as white as you and I. Whether John Scott was the father of the child, I cannot say as she was already pregnant when they got married, but I believe that he was.

But it is not the article, which contains several other errors, that I write this letter to criticize as I have already mentioned. Some of what is in the article is actually true, like in the description of Ann Melton:

"She is apparently about twenty-five years of age, is the illegitimate daughter of one Carlotta Foster, and is a most beautiful woman. She is entirely uneducated, and though living to the midst of depravity and ignorance has the manners and bearing of an accomplished lady, and all the natural powers that should grace a high born beauty."

Maybe a bit exaggerated, but everyone thought she was beautiful. Even those who otherwise despised her had to admit as much. I remember her as being very beautiful as well, although my memory may fail me here, I am after all now more than 65 years old, almost the number counted out in The Holy Book. [Publisher's note: I wondered what the Doctor Carter meant by this, so I looked it up on the internet, and I think that he is referring to this line from Psalms chapter 90 verse 10: *"The days of our years are threescore years and ten"*.] As I have previously told, she was my patient before her arrest, and I treated her and many other unfortunate victims of the terrible disease, syphilis, which ravaged our entire state in the years after the civil war and which is still abounding widely. I also attended the trials and here she actually showed nice manners, although some of my not so well-behaved patients, who had also been present in court, thought she was stuck-up, arrogant and just pretended that she was a lady, even if she herself was just a poor farmer's wife from the countryside, daughter of a woman of low morality and completely without morality herself. And that she definitely was no better than them! They used a much harsher language than this, but I will not indulge in such words as they did. However, the journalist must have spoken to someone who had told him this because there were no journalists from New York in court, neither in 1866 nor in 1868. We had not seen a journalist in our part of the world either, since right after the war had ended. This may be the reason why he did not know much about our ways, but invented most of the story himself.

Life goes on in the hills and the valley

In October 1868 Ann Melton's case was brought to trial in Wilkesboro, and here she was acquitted. I was not present in court as I was not called as a witness, but James Isbell, who was present during the very short trial, later told me that the confession that Thomas Dula had signed and in which he declared that he was the only one responsible for Laura Foster's death, was the major reason for the acquittal. Another reason was that the prosecutor could not find many who would bear testimony against her. Later people who might have been witnesses, explained that there was no reason for them to testify, as they did not believe that any court in North Carolina would convict and hang a white woman. I found that strange though, as almost everybody in the area knew about Frankie Silver, and the song, that was sung about her.

After Ann Melton's release, she returned to her husband and daughter in Elkville, and shortly after, she visited me to resume the treatment that had been discontinued for the more than two years she had spent in jail. She showed no symptoms at the time, but such is this terrible disease. The symptoms disappear quite soon after both the first and second stage of the illness, but the disease can then return in a fatal form many years later. Of course, she would like to avoid that; therefore, she wanted to be treated once more. We resumed treatment, but as she did not show any symptoms like I just told, it was difficult to say if the treatment had any effect. And even if many die from this disease and a terrible death at that, quite a few survive even without treatment.

Both before and after Ann Melton's trial and release from prison, life went on in Happy Valley and in the hills surrounding the valley. Everyone tried to recover from the trials of war. Many had lost family members, and many of those who had returned from the war were marked by their experiences, both on body and soul. Nevertheless, times improved just a little over the following years. Some of those who suffered the hardest were the former slaves, who now had to feed themselves, which was not that easy, as they had difficulties earning money to buy food and other necessities. A few left the area and traveled north, but some remained and some of those who did travel north, returned disappointed. They had thought that they would be received with open arms by the northerners, but that was not even close to the truth. Most northerners did not want the black people to come and compete with them for jobs. Anyway there had never been that many slaves in Happy Valley, only about 90 in total also counting children and a couple of years after the war there were about 60 black people left in the area. Many of these had to accept jobs with their previous owners, but now they were paid wages, though very little and the majority had troubles providing for themselves. Many therefore accepted to become sharecroppers, where the payment was none, but where they were allowed to keep some of what they grew for their former master, and at least were able to put some food on their tables. Also many white people from the hills had to choose this way of making a living. Some had been sharecroppers already before the war, while some now had to resort to this little lucrative occupation in order to survive.

Even I could feel that many were under a financial strain, as it became harder and harder for me to get people to pay for the treatments they received. Not that they did not want to, but they simply could not afford it. This did not change until the late 1870s, when the tide finally turned in the valley. As a doctor though, I felt an obligation to help anyway, and fortunately I owned some fertile land in the valley and also some not so fertile in the hills. This remote land was run by a couple of sharecroppers, among which was Francis Melton, a brother of Ann Melton's husband, James. Besides from making a living from this land, Francis Melton and two more sharecroppers also helped running my land in the valley. Especially this fertile soil in the vicinity of the river provided a good income, and when my father-in-law died five years before the civil war, my wife had inherited a sum of money, though not that much as all the 14 siblings had to divide the estate and the personal property between them, but at least we could get by, even if I treated a lot of my patients for free. Many were grateful and if they managed to earn some money, most offered to pay for my services later, which I normally turned down.

Among those who had to give up was Mary Dula, Thomas Dula's mother. She tried to run her farm on her own for a couple of years, but she was rather old, actually older than I am today, and hadn't as much energy as before. Although both men and women in this rural area of the state are hardy, it became too much for her with no menfolk to help and a daughter, that did not walk very well. When it came to the point where she wanted to sell her property, I offered to buy her house and the rather large tract of land that she had inherited from her husband. I offered a reasonable sum, although there was only a little fertile soil while most of the land was forested hills. This offer she accepted with gratitude. She and her daughter, Eliza, who had

had an accident, when she was a little girl, an accident, that she never fully recovered from, finally moved in with the family of Mary Dula's oldest daughter, Anna Hendrix, who lived and still lives in the local area close to Linville Branch. [Publishers note: I couldn't find Linville Branch on a modern day map, but discovered that the name has since been changed to Laytown Creek.] Mary had two other daughters. One was Sarah, who had been married before I arrived in the area and had moved to Lenoir in Caldwell County. Mary didn't want to move in with her as she could not "live in a big city", as she told me when we finished the deal. And that even though there were fewer than 500 people living in Lenoir and even today, almost 20 years later, there are just a little over 600. The fourth daughter, Selena, also got married before I got to Happy Valley, and after her marriage she moved to Georgia with her husband and that was much too far away in Mary Dula's opinion. Although she, like me, was born in Virginia, she moved to Watauga County with her parents as a little girl, and this western part of our state had now become her home as it has become mine, and here she wanted to live for the rest of her life, close to the graves of her husband and her youngest son. And so she did, as she passed away only last year at the ripe age of 86, while still living in the home of her oldest daughter, Anna.

I found a married couple whose children had grown up and had left home to settle for themselves. The couple accepted to work as sharecroppers on my land against being allowed to live in the former Dula home, which was relatively large for a house in the hills, where the cabins usually only had a single room. Mary Dula's cabin had two rooms and two lean-to outbuildings, and there was also a barn some distance away and an outhouse just behind the cabin itself. I promised them that all that they could get out of the land that used to belong to Mary Dula, they could keep for themselves and, as always when you hire sharecroppers, I provided tools as I was obliged to do and the family also got a cow that could give them milk and a horse to pull the plow as I didn't have any oxen to spare. Both husband and wife proved themselves to be skilled farmers, and I later considered letting them buy the house and land on favorable conditions, but before they could accept, the husband suddenly died and his wife had no other options than to leave the place and move in with her son who had settled in McDowell County not far from Marion. Since then the cabin has been empty, while I have grown the fields with the help of day laborers.

A confession

Something had long bothered me about Thomas Dula's trial. During the trial that lasted two full days in the first place, my friend and neighbor, James Isbell, explained in his testimony that he had ensured that the prosecutor could hire two assistants, one of which was the already well-known and highly esteemed lawyer, Nathaniel Boyden, who would later defend Governor Holden in his impeachment trial when he was accused of abuse of power in his actions against the strange organization known as Ku Klux Klan. The other was a friend of mine, John Clement, whom I had gotten acquainted with during my stay with the Cowles' family in 1850 and 1851 before moving to Happy Valley. He was now a lawyer in Mocksville in Davie County, neighboring Iredell, but the chief prosecutor chose him, because he did not want a local lawyer from Statesville, as the defense team already employed a lawyer from that town, Mr. Richard M. Allison, and Mr. Caldwell, the prosecutor, thought that he would be too closely connected to either of the other two lawyers in Statesville. That James Isbell paid for these assistants surprised me a lot, and also many others in the community wondered why he did that. I tried to get him to tell me, but with no luck. He just repeated the explanation he had given in court, that he did it for the public good, not because he felt any animosity against Thomas Dula. When I pointed out that he had not shown the same sense of responsibility for the common good in other cases, he completely stopped talking and, in order not to ruin our friendship, after all our wives were cousins and we were neighbors, I left it at that.

After the trial and Thomas Dula's hanging, rumors began to spread rapidly in the neighborhood. It was also a persistent rumor that Mr. Dula had murdered Laura Foster that had led to his arrest in the first place, but now the rumors turned in the opposite direction. Thomas Dula was completely innocent of the crime. Ann Melton had killed Laura Foster in a fit of jealousy, and Pauline Foster had helped her. As Thomas truly loved Ann Melton, he had helped her bury the body. Other rumors would know that Ann Melton had lured a young man from the neighborhood to do the crime for her against promises of her favors, because in that way she could prove that she had been in her home at the time of the murder. In a short while Ann Melton and, in part, Pauline Foster became the villains and Thomas Dula the innocent victim. At the same time, in other versions of the story, Laura Foster's reputation also began to change. Now, she had been a young and innocent girl who had been deceived terribly by Thomas Dula who had promised her marriage in order to lure her first into bed, and later to Bates Place, where either he or Ann Melton had killed her instead. That there was not much truth behind this rumor I knew, because I had treated Laura and Pauline Foster for syphilis weeks before Tom and later Ann approached me with the same disease. Laura was certainly not innocent in the Biblical sense. She was actually known in the neighborhood and in neighboring communities like Elkville, as someone who by a local expression was "a girl with round heels". Most, if not everyone around, knew that she was fond of men and did not need much wooing before she surrendered her virtue or what little was left of it.

I did not believe any of these rumors. Ann Melton was kind of different from other women in the hills, that is true, and she often acted like she was better than her peers, and she was also known to be hot tempered and sometimes even aggressive if she did not get things her way, but even so I did not perceive her as someone who would kill anyone. Rather, she would have enjoyed being able to steal Laura's lover away from her and then gloat about it. It was a little different with Pauline, but neither, I thought, had committed the murder. Pauline was not at all like that, even though she could be in awful mood at times and it is true nobody really know what people can do if they are put under pressure, but I do not think that Pauline was under any kind of pressure that might have driven her to murder. In addition, Pauline explained in court that she had worked in the field with James Melton and a day laborer called Jonathan Gilbert at the time that the prosecutor believed the murder had taken place, which was confirmed by James Melton.

In court several witnesses testified that Ann Melton spent almost all the day that Laura disappeared in her bed and did not get up until evening. No, I was quite sure that Thomas Dula was the guilty one, and that he was also rightfully convicted and hanged, though I really did not understand what could be his reason for killing Laura – definitely not the syphilis as claimed by the prosecutor and not the pregnancy claimed by the newspaper reporter. This I explained to everybody when we got to talk about the case. On the other hand, Ann Melton apparently knew where the body was buried as she had led Pauline Foster to the place, or if Pauline had lied about this in court, she must have known herself, for in the end it was she who showed the sheriff and the search party to the general area in which the grave was. But I soon stopped wondering as I had more important things to think about, like taking care of Juliet, our two surviving children and my patients.

Ann and James Melton, who were both infected with syphilis, used to visit me for treatment, but never together, always only the one of them. The treatment was not very pleasant though as I used blue mass and blue stone, but it seemed to work as it sometimes does, while at other times and with other patients it does not. [Publisher's note: I had to do some research into these remedies. What was blue mass and blue stone? Well, I discovered that blue mass was a remedy consisting of at least 33 % mercury and some crushed plants like marshmallow and a little bit of glycerin, and often used for people infected with syphilis, as it kills bacteria, and apparently even Abraham Lincoln was a frequent user, even if nobody knows what ailment he used it against. Mercury is poisonous and can affect your brain creating changes in behavior, and in the end be fatal, so maybe you are cured of the disease only to be killed by the medication. Blue stone is copper sulfate that was normally used as an emetic, so why the good doctor used that, I have no idea. But also copper sulfate is very poisonous and is not used anymore for the same reason, so there was a good chance that the patient would die from the treatment, if they were not lucky. But I'll let the doctor continue.] But one day, after the treatment had stopped, they both arrived together and they were looking very happy when they entered my office. They told me that they thought Ann was pregnant, which pleased them both. Their oldest daughter, Martha Jane, was now 9 years old and they would like to have more children which had been prevented by first the war, and then her long imprisonment. In 1871, Ann gave birth to a daughter and they named her Ida, a beautiful child, who reminded me of my own two daughters when they were born.

However, it turned out that the child was somewhat weak, so I often visited their home, just as they came to me to get her examined. I can add though that she is 16 years old today and thrives well, but when little she was an ailing child.

About one year after Ida had been born to the Meltons, James Isbell came to visit. He came to tell me and Juliet that his wife, Sarah Louise, was pregnant again with the family's fourth child. He seemed happy though very quiet, and not in as good a mood as I would have expected. And when we had talked for a while, he asked for a word with me in private, so we went into my office. I explained to him that there was nothing to worry about as Sarah Louise had born their first three children completely without complications. I can add that she is now the mother of seven children, each one was born without any complications either. However, that was not what worried him.

When I asked him what it was, he became very nervous and referred to the question I had asked several years ago about why he was so keen on having Thomas Dula convicted. I remembered this with absolute clarity, and now it appeared as if I would finally get the explanation that he had for so long kept to himself.

"Do you remember," he asked, "when Sarah was pregnant with Mary in the first year of the war?"

Mary was their second child and the oldest daughter and she was born in the spring of 1862, when the war was one-year-old. Of course, I remembered as I had helped bringing the girl into this world because the midwife was busy elsewhere and could not get there in time. His next words shocked me, though they should not have when I think of it now.

"I'm not Mary's father," he declared.

"What do you mean?" was my reaction.

"When was Mary born?"

"In the spring of 1862 in the second year of the war," was my answer. "

"Exactly! And when did I enroll in the Confederate army?"

Suddenly a light dawned upon me. James had joined the army in May 1861, and therefore could not be the father of a child born almost one year later. I must have looked as shocked as I felt, because he continued.

"I'm sure that the scoundrel, Thomas Dula is the father. He always visited us, even though he had nothing to do at our place, and I tried to get him to leave, but Sarah said he was family, and seemed to enjoy his company and especially his attention. I'm sure he kept coming at her, after I left for the army.

"But he was only 16," I replied.

"Yes but that does not mean anything. He was a tall and good looking guy, and Sarah was definitely not the first woman, not even the first married woman, he had charmed."

When I asked him if he had talked to Sarah about it, he explained that she had at first refused to have been with any other man but him, but of course in the end she had to acknowledge that unless she had had a very long pregnancy, James could not be the father, and she admitted her unfaithfulness. She claimed that she had felt lonely and in need of a man, but she would not tell James who it was and strongly denied that it was her five-year younger second cousin. Maybe she feared what James would do to the man in question. James had not believed her though, and when Thomas Dula was arrested for the murder of Laura Foster, a murder he, like me, was convinced that Dula had actually committed, he had taken the opportunity to "get revenge for Tom making him a cuckold" as he said.

"So when Tom Dooley told at the gallows that you and Carlotta Foster and her son, Thomas had committed perjury, in your case he hinted at your testimony about not feeling any enmity towards him, but only did what you did for the sake of the public good?"

Thomas Dula never mentioned at the gallows, what James had committed perjury about, even if he said that Carlotta and Thomas Foster had lied about his whereabouts on that Friday.

"Yes, it cannot have been anything else".

"But how did he know that?"

"Because I confronted him when he returned from the prisoner of war camp, telling him to stay far away from Sarah Louise in the future, or else I would take my precautions!"

"And what did he answer?"

"He did not deny that they had a relationship, nor did he promise to stay away, but I did not see him on my farm after that."

"Did he confirm the relationship?"

"He would not talk about it, and that made me sure I was right."

"And now you're nervous if Sarah has been with someone else again?" I asked. "Have you any reason to believe that the child she is expecting now is not yours?"

James shook his head, but did not answer. I was sure he suspected that his wife had been unfaithful to him once again, but I was as sure that she had not, now that he had returned from the war and also from Congress duty several years ago.

"And how about Thomas?"

James left the army in 1862, when he was elected for the legislative assembly where he served, first as a congressman later as a senator. Thomas was their third child, born in 1864 while

James was a member of the North Carolina Congress in Raleigh, "Do you think you're not his father either?"

"No I'm sure that Sarah became pregnant right before I left for Raleigh or on my visit home after a month. And he looks like me, while Mary does not look anything like neither me nor Sarah."

"But why do you tell me this story right now when you did not want to relate it before?" was my next question.

He sat silent for a long time with his head bent before answering without looking up.

"Because now I have made another woman pregnant myself, and that while Sarah is pregnant as well, and I blame myself for what I have done. What will it do to our marriage? I still love my wife very much in spite of all that she and I have done."

This time I was not too surprised. Many of the wealthy plantation owners in the valley had children out of wedlock, often with former slaves, as some of them still felt they had a right to sleep with those girls. But before I could ask who the mother was, he continued himself:

"It's Eliza Anderson,"

he said, and now I was surprised. Eliza Anderson was a member of the respectable Anderson clan whose head was Sarah Anderson, known as Sallie, a widow who was about 55 years old, and many in the area had great sympathy for her because of the way she had raised her family and taken care of her farm after her husband had passed away far too early. The family belonged to the poor part of the population and they lived at that time in the hills near Reedy Branch not far from where Ann Melton and Tom Dooley lived, but later the family moved to Stoney Fork a bit further north. Several of her children, including the only one married at the time of the murder, Celia Scott, had been witnesses during the trial against Thomas Dula. Her youngest son, George Washington Anderson, who served in the army with Thomas Dula, was probably Dula's best friend, and Eliza, her second youngest daughter, was only 18 years old in 1871, when the events that I am here referring to took place.

It did not really surprise me that a pretty young girl who could probably get any young man, still would lie with a man twice her own age, because many of the poor girls in the area slept with older and richer men, most in the hope of gaining some favors.

"Have you told Sarah?" I asked, but he denied.

"You will have to do that," I said.

"She admitted her mistake to you, so you must at least do the same for her. And you must take responsibility for the child and acknowledge for the records if not to the world that you are the father."

He nodded without looking up, and soon after, we said goodbye, and I told him to go home and get it over with. I do not know if he did it right away, but when the child was born, he accepted the paternity which was stated on the child's birth certificate. The child was called Simpson Anderson and James supported Eliza while the boy was little. He is 15 years old now and works as a farm laborer for Larkin Horton, James Isbell's brother-in-law and I am sure James has seen to that.

Sarah Louise must have accepted the relationship because she's still with James and as I said before, they have had three more children after the one Sarah was bearing at the time. For some reason they named him Robert Lee Isbell after the famous general and my own second cousin who had passed away two years before James' son was born. [Publisher's note: My research shows that Dr. Carter actually was a second cousin of Confederate General Robert E. Lee, as the doctor's father was a cousin of the general's mother, Ann Hill Carter Lee.] The youngest of their children is James, whom they call "Little Jim", and he is only seven years old as I write this. No one in the Isbell family ever mentions Simpson or says anything about Mary being illegitimate, sired by Thomas Dula or whoever it may be, because Sarah Isbell has never revealed who the father of Mary actually is, not to James, not to me or Juliet while she was still alive. However, I have someone else in mind, as I think Mary has an astonishing likeness of this man's daughters but since I cannot prove it, I've always kept it to myself, and I am not about to change that now. Eliza Anderson is still unmarried but now she is the mother of three children; besides Simpson she also has a son and a daughter. The son is called James Gaither, and his father is my wife's cousin, Rufus Dula Horton; and Rufus is also the father of Eliza's daughter, Alverty. He seems very fond of Eliza even if he will not marry her, at least not this far.

Ann Melton's secret

A rumor that started soon after Ann Melton's tragic death and still goes around, claimed that on her deathbed she told me a secret, a secret that could have saved Thomas Dula from the gallows but that she made me swear to keep silent forever. This rumor soon evolved into a whole story and ended up with Ann Melton confessing to me that she had murdered Laura Foster in jealousy over her relationship, not only with Tom but with Ann's husband, James as well. She had then cynically allowed her lover go to the gallows in her place because of him sleeping with Laura Foster. I am sure that one of the old "witches" who flocked to Mrs. Melton's deathbed like vultures that flock around a carcass, was who created this rumor. It may have been the old gossip, Betsy Watson, who I know was the one who spread the rumor that Ann was on her way to Hell, and that you could actually see the flames of Hell on the walls, hear the sound of sizzling meat and see cats crawling on Anne's body just before she drew her final breath. *"That was when The Devil himself came to claim her evil soul,"* were the words Betsy used, when she later recounted this story. But the story of the confession could also have originated from one of the three or four other old hags that were present. Apologies, but even now, almost 15 years later, I still do not like the way they acted then. But I have never shown it in public of course, as I am their physician as well. The only one I do not actually suspect is Carlotta Foster, Ann's mother, and it's because I know that she knew, who actually killed Laura Foster, and I know that too and have since 1873. Apart from the killer and Carlotta Foster I am the only person alive who know the truth. And neither the killer nor Mrs. Foster will ever tell, because they would most likely both be hanged if they did. One for the killing and the other for assisting in hiding the crime. In fact, this is what has caused me to tell this story, although I do not want it to be published until after all those involved have passed away. I owe that to myself, Ann Melton and to all the other people who were involved in the story. It is far too late to provide justice for Thomas Dula, and although he would definitely be acquitted, he probably does not care where he is now; hopefully in a better world than this one, if such a place exists which I doubt. No, I tell the story which is weighing on my own conscience, as I have kept the story to myself for so many years, but I gave a solemn promise at the time and I will keep it until my death and for many years after that.

But I must stress here that Ann Melton told me absolutely nothing on her deathbed. She was simply not able to. One day, when she was on her way home after a visit to Cowles' Store, she had an accident. As I told you before, the store was still known under that name, even if my old acquaintance Calvin Cowles, to whom I will forever be grateful for introducing me to Juliet, had sold it years ago before the war. Ann Melton was riding in an ox cart that James Melton had built. He was a skilled craftsman and worked as a cooper and a wagon maker as well as a carpenter and cobbler. The cart was pulled by one of the family's three milk cows, as they did not own any draft animals. While on her way home, the cart hit a bump in the road and turned over. This happened on Stony Fork Road not far from her mother's home. The cart fell so unfortunate that she was caught under it, and James Melton had built the cart not only strong but also very heavy. I was told that she screamed so loudly from the pain that many people came running from the nearest fields and houses. They moved the cart from her and carried her home to Carlotta Foster's little cabin while her younger sister, Martha, was sent to fetch me. When I reached the cabin she was pale and her forehead was moist with cold sweat. The only sounds she made were some low moans. I sent everyone out of the little single room cabin while I examined her.

It's probably the time I spent alone with her that caused the rumors of her confession, because I was not alone with her at any time after that. She could not have told me anything though, as soon after I began my examination of her, she lost her consciousness. From that time either her husband, her brother Thomas, her younger sister, Martha, or her mother was by her side to her last moment, and Martha Jane, her own oldest daughter, 12 years old at the time was present most of the time. I do not think that the daughter slept at all for several days. In addition, the aforementioned "witches" were just outside and sometimes inside the cabin, as well as several other neighbors who came, some to satisfy their curiosity, others rather to ask whether they could be of any help.

Already during my first examination, I realized that she was beyond medical help. Something was bleeding inside her and I was almost certain that it was her liver, that had been damaged, but I could not say for sure without opening her, and I did not dare; I do not hesitate to admit that. However, I was in no doubt that she had internal hemorrhages, and all I could do was to pray for the bleeding to stop by itself. I therefore told her relatives that if she woke up, she could not have anything to eat or drink, but they could moisten her lips when they became too dry. The next day I visited again, but if her condition had changed it was for the worse; she was still unconscious. On the third day I was sent for again by her younger sister, Martha, who asked me to come as quickly as possible, which I did. But it was in vain. When I reached Carlotta Foster's cabin, Ann Melton had already drawn her final breath. It was on that occasion that I first heard the story of what had happened just before she died, The Devil coming to get her and all. As it was summer and very hot, she was buried the very next day on a plot close to her mother's cabin. Later other members of the Melton family have found their last resting place there as well.

But let me get back to how I found out who had killed Laura Foster and why. One day, during one of my visits to the Melton family to care for Ida, who was again ailing, James Melton was not at home. On this day he used his skills as a carpenter to help one of the plantation owners in the valley build a new barn after the old one had been washed away by a flood when the Yadkin River, as so often before had flooded the lower parts of the valley. When I finished the examination, Ann's oldest daughter, Martha Jane, who was also present, took Ida home to her grandmother's cabin, a few hundred yards away, and I made ready to go home when Ann grabbed my arm. I will give the following conversation between us as close to what was actually said as I remember it, but some words can be wrong, as fourteen years has passed since it took place. What was said shocked me so much though, that most is still fresh in my memory.

"Is it true Doctor that a doctor cannot tell anyone what a patient has told him?"

I looked a little surprised at her.

"I think you are confusing a doctor with a minister, but it is true that as a doctor I do not discuss my patients' diseases with other people unless it is necessary to help, and then only with another doctor. But why do you want to know? "

She apparently did not know whether to answer or stay silent, but eventually she looked up.

"There is something I would like to tell someone, but no-one except from the one I tell must ever know, and we have no priest here about, and I thought that maybe I could tell you."

"Well, I am not a priest, but the circuit rider will get here in a month or two, and you can talk to him."

"I cannot wait for that. My eternal soul is in danger and we never know when The Good Lord becomes impatient and picks us up."

If she had known how prophetic this statement would prove to be, she probably would not have made it but fortunately, she could not predict the future although some of the neighbors later thought she had been a witch.

"You can tell your story to me, and I promise not to tell it to anyone," I said, "but then you must also tell the minister when he arrives."

"I will do that, but if I tell you the story, you'll have to swear on your life, and on the lives of your loved ones never to tell a single soul what you hear."

I promised her, but she fetched the family Bible and asked me to put my hand on it and swear a solemn oath that for as long as I lived, I would never let a living soul know what she was about to tell me. I did as she asked, and when I now break this oath with this letter, I may lose my immortal soul, but I will also lose it if I do not tell the story, if a man has an immortal soul to lose that is. And by entrusting my knowledge to a distant future when I am no longer walking this earth, I have not truly broken my oath, and I therefore hope that I will escape from Purgatory, if such a thing exists. I am not a Catholic and do not believe in those kind of things. In fact, I'm not particularly a believer at all. My beloved daughter, Julia, who was only seven months old when taken from us in 1857, was buried in the Dula-Horton family cemetery near the old home of Juliet's grandparents, Captain William and his wife Theodocia Dula. This family cemetery is not connected to any particular denomination as different members of the family had different beliefs. After Mariah Ernest had a small chapel built very close to my home a few years ago, the first church in Happy Valley actually, I have visited this at long intervals. This chapel belongs to the Methodist denomination, which Mariah Ernest herself belonged to, and so did most of the circuit riders that came to our community, but I am neither Methodist, Baptist, Presbyterian nor am I anything else. I believe in the existence of a higher power, but not one who interferes with our lives, and not one who punishes us either before or after death. The punishments before death we take pretty well care of ourselves, and ... well, I do not think there's anything left after we have died, no afterlife whatsoever, but please do not let a priest read this. And, in spite of my lack of belief, my dear Juliet is buried in the small cemetery surrounding the chapel that Miss Ernest have had built, and when I pass I shall be buried next to her.

After having sworn on the Bible, I was asked to sit down as Mrs. Melton fetched a jug of water from the well outside and two cups. And then she began to talk.

> "Tom did not kill Laurie Foster. He had nothing to do with the murder at all. And neither did he help me nor anyone else bury Laurie's body"

I must have looked suspicious because she continued:

> "No, Doctor. It was not me either. I know the rumors going around about me being the killer, but I was not. And neither was Purlene as some believe."

As I have mentioned before, Pauline Foster, Ann's distant cousin was at the time of the murder working as a farm laborer and if Ann had her will – which she, according to what Pauline had told me during her consultations, often did – also as a housekeeper in the Melton household. But now I could not keep quiet any longer:

> "But if it was not Thomas Dula, Pauline Foster or yourself, then who was it? And how did you know where the grave was? Or how did Pauline know, if she told a lie in court about you showing her where the grave was?"

"She did not tell a lie, Doctor. I showed her the way to the grave, but she got scared and did not want to follow me all the way."

"Is it true what she told in court that if the grave was disturbed, you would dig up the body and bury it again in your own cabbage piece? Or cut it into pieces and throw the pieces into the pigsty?"

"It's correct. I told her so, but the grave was not disturbed, so it did not matter."

"But if none of you had anything to do with the murder, why would you commit such disgusting acts"? Would you really have done that?"'

"I would Doctor Carter, I really would. Yes, I would surely have done it."

"But why?"

"If I can just tell my story, you will realize why."

I thought that I should rather let her talk without interruptions. I could always ask more questions when she was done. Then she continued:

"On the day Laurie Foster left her home, she was going to meet someone at Bates Place that same morning, but it was not Tom. Either Betsy Scott lied in court or Laurie had lied to her when they met that Friday morning, and I believe that Laura did lie to Betsy, as she wanted no-one to know who she was really going to meet! I know it was not Tom she was meeting, because he, Mom and I, had been out in the woods all night and had shared a large canteen of moonshine, which Tom's cousin Carson had brought us in the afternoon. Carson makes the best liquor in this part of Wilkes County, I think. Neither Tom, nor mom or I were feeling well in the morning but Tom suffered the most as he had drunk more than me and mom, and when mom went back to her cabin I know that Tom returned to his own home long before dawn, as I followed him a bit along the way before I returned to my own home, where I arrived around an hour or so before daybreak. Before we kissed goodbye that morning, Tom promised me that he would meet me again the very next evening.

Once again I interrupted her story with a question.

"But Calvin Carlton and Hezekiah Kendall both testified in court, that they had met Mr. Dula on the path from German hill to Reedy Branch on that morning. Why would they lie about that?"

"I do not think Mr. Carlton really lied Doctor. I am sure the two of them actually had met Tom, on the path but it was not on that morning. If what Tom told me at another time, weeks before he was arrested is true, he had met them on one of his first visits to Laurie's home, when he used the narrow path instead of the river road in order to avoid meeting the father of Linny Barnes, who was very angry with him, as he thought that Tom had seduced his daughter. The reason Tom told me this was that he actually bragged about other men being jealous of his success with women. So I think that Mr. Carlton simply got things mixed up. Maybe Hezekiah lied about it though. He was not married then and was quite interested in Laurie himself, so maybe he wanted to harm Tom, and when he found out that Mr. Carlton remembered the date wrong, he just changed his own testimony to fit that."

I doubted that someone could remember several weeks wrong, but did not question her further on the matter and just asked her to go on with her story.

Tom had to get up early on that Friday morning even with his headache and all, because he was to meet Wash Anderson before 8 am. He told me they were going to meet in the home of Celia Scott, to do a bit of hunting on the ridge, but Wash had not been there when Tom arrived. [Publishers note: "Wash" must have been a nickname for George Washington Anderson, who was the younger brother of Celia Scott and as the doctor mentioned above, Tom Dooley's best friend.] He never found him, at least not in the morning and did not want to go hunting alone with his headache and all, so after his visit to Celia Scott, he came to our cabin. He told me that he had been looking for Wash and told me, that he was not feeling well and would go back to his own home and get some sleep, but he would come to visit me that night when James and Purlene had gone to bed. My mom told me later that on his way from my place to his own, he had stopped at her cabin to get some milk, and she had seen him continue towards his mom's cabin.

He did not come to visit in the evening though, because he was still sick when evening came. He left his mother's house, while his mother was preparing supper and began to walk up the path between Mary Dula's cabin and my mother's place, but felt unwell, and therefore returned to his home, and stayed in his mother's cabin for the rest of the night. And that was a good thing, as Friday night both Wilson Foster, my brother Thomas, and Will Holder visited our house, and we drank quite a bit more liquor with Purlene and James also being there, so Tom and I would not have been able to spend time together anyway."

I must have looked impatient because she continued:

"I'm sorry, Doctor. I will go on and get to the point, but there's so much I want to tell you. I do not know who Laurie was really going meet, but I think it was someone from the valley. Early in the morning, my sister, Martha, and my two oldest brothers, who still lived at home, left the cabin to do some work. Thomas had to drop corn with Martha, just like James and Purlene, while Pinkney had other chores to do closer to the cabin. You know that when he returned from the war Pinkney moved back in with mother, and stayed there until he had built his own cabin a couple of years later and moved there. Mom stayed in the cabin with Linny and Marshall, my youngest siblings. What they were doing I do not know, as Martha only told me later, that they did not come out, while she and Thomas was working in the field.

As you heard yourself in court, Thomas explained that he had seen Tom go by in the direction of the Scott home, but that is not true. I was told that Tom said at the gallows that Thomas, my brother, had lied about Tom's whereabouts that day, and that was true. Thomas never saw Tom, but Martha did, and she saw him walking in the direction of James and Celia Scott's home. Much later she told Thomas this, and as he wanted Tom convicted, he changed the story a bit when he testified in court.

I can see from the look on your face, that you wonder why Thomas did not see Tom? Well, Thomas was not there, when Tom walked by mom's cabin! When Laurie rode past my mother's cabin a short while earlier, Thomas called for her, but she just rode on. I do not say that Thomas was in love with Laurie, because he was not, but he definitely was interested in her and wanted to lie with her. Of course, he knew the rumors that she was easy to talk into lifting her skirts for men, and thought that she would lie with him as well if he asked her. When she did not reply to his yells, he told Martha to take a break, and then he followed Laurie which was not difficult for him as she rode bareback and at the same time had to hold on to her bundle of clothes, so she kept a slow speed. When she reached Bates Place, she pulled the horse across the small field surrounding the abandoned shop and into the woods.

Thomas followed her, and saw that she had tied the horse to a tree, and had her back turned against him. He therefore snuck up on her from behind and put his arms around her grabbing for her breasts, causing her to panic and start screaming, so he put his hand over her mouth. She turned around, and when she discovered who it was, she calmed down again but was very angry and asked him what he wanted. He told her he wanted to lie with her, causing her to laugh out loud and accuse him of being just a silly child, and she would only offer her favors to real men. This made Thomas very furious, so he grabbed her and tried to kiss her. But she pulled a knife out of her dress and pointed it at him. He tried to grab the knife, and it came to a fight, and during this Laurie was stabbed in the chest with the knife by accident. She fell to the ground, and he could see that she bled from the chest and with a low voice she asked him for help, but he panicked and ran away from the place and went back to the field where he had been working and acted as if nothing had happened, even if he had to hide his guilt and nervousness from Martha. Our older brother, Pinkney, was at the time Thomas left the field busy chopping wood behind the cabin, so he never noticed that Thomas had been gone. Did you know by the way that my brother Pinkney had served in the army with James, my husband, during the war?"

The last remark seemed unrelated to the story she was telling, but she continued.

Later in the day Thomas returned to the place where he left Laurie and found her dead. Thomas, even though he was only 17 at that time, knew he was in big trouble. He therefore covered the body with branches and moved the horse to another place in the woods, so that its whinny would not draw attention to the place where Laurie's body was hidden.

In the evening Thomas borrowed a horse from a man who was at that time visiting my mother; I do not know which man, because she had more than one lover come calling on her from time to time. He rode up to my home to tell me what had happened, but with all the people in the cabin he could not. Not least because Laurie's father was also present. The next day he told mom instead. She did not particularly like Laurie, but she loved Thomas, so she decided to help. Two days later, or rather two nights later, when Pinkney was staying overnight with Lucinda Dula, you know the widow of Tom's brother, William, whom Pinkney later married and is still married to, mother got Martha to go with her and Thomas, my brother, not Tom Dula, and then they all went up to the place where he had left Laurie's body, and with the help of a blanket tied to a pole they carried it across the ridge and down to Reedy Branch. From there they stayed in the creek to be make sure that they did not leave any tracks. Where they were able to get out of the creek with most ease, they carried the body up the hillside to the place where it was later found. Here they dug a grave that was not big enough, but they did not have time for more, as it was already beginning to dawn. They buried Laurie and returned home and promised each other never to tell anyone. And the next day my mother threw the knife in the river and it was never found again."

She paused for a moment, and I used the opportunity to ask how she knew?

"My younger sister, Martha, was just 12 years old at that time, just like my own Martha Jane is today. When they went to bury the body, mom made Thomas tell her, all that had happened, and of course Martha heard as well, but being as young as she was, she could not keep it to herself. Fortunately, she only told me. She was always pretending to know more than she did, so she would seem more interesting than she really was, so at first I did not believe her, but she said she could prove it and then she took me to the place where they buried Laurie. At that time the grass on the grave was still withered after the turf having been removed and put back, so I had to believe her. I explained to her that she could never to talk to a single person about this ever again except for me, because then mom, Thomas and herself as well would all end up in the gallows. She understood, and I am sure that the thought of everybody including herself being hanged scared her so much that she has never talked about it again.

About a month later, when people had almost stopped the search for Laurie, I became afraid that the grave would be discovered by accident as it was not that far up the hillside, and I knew that Mrs. Dula was grazing her cows in that area which belonged to her. This was actually why mom found that it would be a good place to bury Laurie's body, as it was quite a distance from her own home and if the body was ever found, someone else would be suspected. I believe that she hoped that Tom would be suspected, as she did not like neither him nor his mother and sister very much and even now, when Tom is dead she still despises Mary and Eliza, I think out of envy, because Mary owns her own land while mom does not. Now I wanted to go out there and see if the grave was still undisturbed. It was on that occasion that I had Purlene follow along, but without telling her, how I knew that Laurie was buried there. She was well aware that I had not murdered Laurie but also that I knew who did; therefore, she was trying to get the information from me, not only on this occasion, but several times later as well. It led to many quarrels between us, including the fight that Celia Scott mentioned in court. This was the first time Purlene had mentioned my knowledge of the murder in the presence of other people, and I got very angry and beat her with my walking stick, and I admit that I even tried to strangle her to make her keep quiet. I was so mad at her that I even accused her of having slept with her own brother, Joseph, which I knew that she had not! I told Purlene that if she did not stop talking about the murder around people, she would send herself to the gallows, and that was when she claimed that I was as deep in the mud as she was in the mire, just like Celia Scott testified. And yes, I did tell Celia, that she could never repeat what she had heard to anyone, but I did not threaten to kill her".

Mrs. Melton appeared to have nothing more to say after that, but I was not done questioning her.

"But why did you not tell this to the sheriff when he arrested Thomas Dula for the murder?"

"I could not send my mother, brother and sister to the gallows. That's why I wanted to get rid of the body if I found that it might have threatened their safety."

"But I thought you loved Dula?"

"I did and had since we were young, so yes, I did love him but blood is thicker than water and I loved my family even more, even if other people think that I love only myself.

There was something that had been on my mind asking her, even before Laurie Foster disappeared, when she and Thomas Dula both came to seek treatment for their disease. So now I got my chance, and I took it.

"When you and Thomas Dula first came to seek treatment, did you really believe that Thomas had been infected by Laura Foster and then given you the disease as Mr. Caldwell claimed in court?"

"No, Sir! And Tom did not think he had gotten the disease from Laurie either. I knew I had gotten it from Tom or James as they were the only two men I bedded at that time. But Tom had actually been with a lot of women. Besides Laurie Foster he had been with Purlene and as I told you also with that tarty little slut, Linny Barnes who sees herself so high and mighty just because her father is wealthy, and quite a few others, some married some not, and he knew that anyone of those could have given him the disease."

I found that her remark about Caroline Barnes being "high and mighty" was exactly what other people in the area thought about Mrs. Melton herself, just not with the comment of her father being wealthy, as nobody except maybe for her mother, knew who her father was. But I did not comment on that.

"But what about the claim that he had threatened to kill Laura for being the one who had infected him, as Mr. Hall mentioned in court?

"If you remember Doctor, that was not what Rufe Hall actually said. He said that Tom had threatened to "put through" those who had given him the disease, He said that in anger, like you know you can do when you are angry about something, like when I sometimes say to Martha Jane, that I will kill her, if she does not do her chores. It was Mr. Caldwell who made it sound like Tom threatened to kill Laurie, but he did not, as none of us knew from whom Tom had gotten the disease in the first place. I am sure, that James got it from Purlene though, as I did not bed him much after Tom returned from the war." [Publisher's note: My research showed that Walther P. Caldwell, District Attorney for the 6th Judicial District was the chief prosecutor at Tom Dooley's trial.]

"How could you accept that Dula had all these lovers aside from you?"

"Well first of all, Tom accepted that I had seen other men during the war when he and James were away, and I knew that he had seen other women as well, and as I was married I had no right to be jealous. And by the way, I knew Tom well enough to understand, that these women did not mean anything to him. It was only the pursuit and the conquest, that mattered to Tom. Once he had bedded them a couple of times, he lost interest. I was the only one that he loved. Only him bedding Linny Barnes I hated, and we once had an argument about that. She is too pretty and wealthy as well, and she wanted Tom for herself."

I believed that she probably disliked Caroline Barnes because she saw her as maybe the only true competitor to Thomas Dula's favor. But instead of commenting, I just asked something that I had we wondering ever since I learned it during the trials.

"And your husband, James, how could he accept your relationship with Thomas Dula?"

"To tell you the truth Doctor, I do not know. I know that he loved me very much, and you know that people sleeping with someone but their spouse is not that uncommon, at least not in these parts. I even heard that your neighbor, James Isbell, is the father of the child that Eliza Anderson recently gave birth to. So maybe James, my husband James, was just seeing this as the way of life. I know that he himself slept with Purlene quite a few times and I suspect that he also bedded that Gilbert woman, Louisa, who lives in Rufus Hall's household."

She may have been right there. Quite soon after Ann Melton's death, James Melton actually married Louisa Gilbert, who already had an illegitimate daughter when they got married. I do not know who the father of Louisa Gilbert's daughter was, but I do not think it was James Melton, as the daughter, Ellen, stayed with her mother's uncle, when Louisa married James Melton and did not move in with the two of them even if her grandmother and her mother's sister did. I wondered how Mrs. Melton knew that

James Isbell was the father of Eliza Anderson's child, as James, except from recognizing the child in the birth records and helping out the mother in secret, had tried to keep quiet about the affair, but maybe it was Eliza Anderson herself who had told somebody who had then told somebody else and so on. Rumors spread fast in this rural area, so even if James had not told his wife, she would have learned soon enough.

"What about the rumor, that Thomas Dula, not you husband is the father of Martha Jane. Is that true?"

To my surprise she looked down but finally she answered my question. Even if at first I did not believe she was going to tell me.

"To be honest doctor, I do not know. It could be Tom, but it could also very well be James as I lay with both of them at the time I got pregnant if only a few times with James. You know, in spite of what people believe, I do love James but Tom was my first love and lover even if he was younger than me, and I loved him in another way and even more than the love I feel for James."

I did believe her. I do think it is possible to love two people at the same time, no matter what other people may think. I also knew Ann Melton as a woman who in spite of her beauty, had a very low self-esteem and validated herself from the attention she got from other people, especially from men, and she knew no better way to attract men's attention than to sleep with them, especially if she could gain something from it. I do still wonder though why James Melton accepted her affairs with another man though, and even when he was present. The only reason I can think of, is if he himself had an affair with someone other than his wife.

But she continued

"Also I never thought Tom would be convicted if the body was never found, and when he did get convicted, it was too late for me to do anything. At that time, I could not tell what really happened without getting myself into trouble and get arrested with the rest of my family. Later I was arrested anyway because of what Purlene told the sheriff, but at that time I just feared getting sent to jail and later to the gallows and thought that if I just kept quiet, this would not happen. And while I was in jail, I still kept thinking of my family, so I did not even tell then. I also hoped that they would let me go, so I could return to James and my daughter, and I was afraid that it would never happen if I told them what I knew."

"But if Tom was innocent and did not know who killed Laura, why then did he write a confession?"

"He did not write it himself. Allison, the lawyer wrote it for him, or so Mr. Vance told me, and I do not think Tom even knew about it. If he had actually confessed, there was no reason for him to deny his guilt even at the gallows, as I understood that he did"

"But why would Mr. Allison write a confession for Thomas Dula?"

"I think Zebulon Vance and Allison did it for James' sake so that I could be acquitted, as he knew James from the war or perhaps he did it a little for me."

The last part she added with a complacent smile, and I did not know what to answer to this. Had the former governor really betrayed the justice system just to get her acquitted, or was it Allison alone? Or had Ann misunderstood the situation? If she had, I still could not understand why Tom would have confessed – unless it was to save Ann from the gallows, and unfortunately I could not attribute to him such a degree of self-sacrifice.

"Who do you think Laura Foster was going to meet that morning?" I asked, "And why did he not show up?"

"As I said before I do not know who it was, but I have a suspicion that may answer some of your questions if I'm right. Laurie was not only sleeping with men but with women as well. I know because we had slept together on some occasions but please do not tell James that.

I do not know why she asked me not to tell her husband, as I had already sworn on the Bible not to tell anyone, but I guess it was just a remark of the moment, as she was eager that her husband did not found out about her being with another woman. But she continued:

He knows that I have been unfaithful to him, not only with Tom, but with a few more men during the war, but he doesn't know that I have bedded another woman and I think he would divorce me if he knew. I even think that Laurie maybe liked women better than men. That is why I believe that Laurie was supposed to meet a woman from the valley, probably a wealthy woman. I do not know who, but maybe a woman that she had met at one of the dances that took place that spring where she was hired as a server, or maybe someone that she had helped weaving. You remember that Laura was very well known for her weaving skills? Anyway I think that this woman came to the place they had agreed to meet, and there she found Laurie's dead body. As she could not afford to get involved, she left the place again and never said anything to anyone."

"But why did she not say anything when Thomas Dula was accused?"

"She probably thought that it was Tom who had killed Laurie, and if so, she might even have wanted revenge for her lover."

"And you do not know who this woman may be?"

"I do not."

She looked away when she answered and I am sure that she lied to me, and that she at least had a suspicion of who it may have been even if she did not know for sure. Ever since, I have been wondering if it could be true what Ann Melton told me, and if it was, then who could this secretive woman be, but I have never come to any conclusion in the matter. I have my own suspiscion though, that maybe she was meeting with a man after all, and that man could be my neighbor and friend,

James Isbell, which would better explain why he wanted Thomas Dula hanged for the murder, if he actually suspected that he had killed a woman that James himself had an affair with. I never mentioned this suspicion to anyone though and at the time I just asked Mrs. Melton another question:

"In court Pauline Foster testified that your brother Thomas had an argument with Mr. Dula. Do you know what that was about?"

"I was not present at the time, but Purlene told me, that they were quarrelling about her. They both slept with her, and my brother was mad because, Tom slept with me and Purlene, and he wanted Purlene for himself. I do not know though, if Purlene was lying, and just told me this to prove that she had men fighting over her. If she was lying I do not know what else they may have been quarrelling about."

I did not know what else to say or ask at that time. I later I thought of many other questions I should have asked, but I could not get hold of my thoughts at all, so I remained silent for a long time. Eventually we could hear someone on the path outside the cabin, and it turned out that it was James Melton returning home. He wondered why I was there, but I explained that I had been visiting Ida, and that I examined her and also had brought medication for her. James never asked me, why I was still there when Ida had been taken to her grandmother's home, but he probably thought that I had discussed other medical matters with his wife. I took leave and returned to my own home. I had sworn on the Bible, not to tell anyone what I had heard, and that promise I wanted to keep, but I decided to visit

Ann Melton again later to find out more. Unfortunately, I never got to do that as a few days later she was killed in the accident, and I couldn't ask neither Carlotta Foster nor Thomas Foster or Martha Foster. And now it's impossible as Martha died in childbirth sometime in 1877 and her mother, who is still alive even if a couple of years older than me, will definitely not talk about it, and surely neither will Thomas Foster.

Did I believe what Ann Melton told me? Yes I did, and I still do. I first thought she was just trying to clear her lover of his alleged guilt, but if that was the case, why then had she sworn me to silence? Only if I told the story, Thomas Dula would be cleared of blame, but that would bring misery to Mrs. Melton's own family. So I had to believe that she had told me the truth, at least as far as she knew it herself, just to clear her conscience. Exactly the same reason I have to write down this whole sad and tragic story.

A few months after Ann Melton's death, when I was visiting Wilkesboro for some reason that I have long forgotten, I happened to meet John Clement, my lawyer friend who had been prosecuting the case together with the Chief Prosecutor, Mr. Caldwell and Mr. Boyden. [Publisher's note: Nathaniel Boyden was a well-known lawyer of the day. He was elected to the US Senate in 1868 beating Dr. Carter's friend, Calvin Cowles, in the election, and in 1870 he defended governor William Holden in the impeachment trial against him.] John was in town, for a meeting with a lawyer colleague about a completely different case. I told him that I knew for sure that Thomas Dula had not killed Laura Foster. I could not tell him how I knew or who actually did the evil deed, but he could choose to believe me on my word or not. I think he actually did believe me, since from that day forward he has refused to prosecute cases, where the death penalty can be the outcome in case of a guilty verdict. I think he was so shocked to learn that they had convicted and hanged an innocent man that he simply will not risk it again. If he later told the other prosecutors or the judges what I told him, I do not know.

Some months later I also tried to tell James Isbell that I knew for certain that Thomas Dula did not kill Laura Foster, but he didn't want to listen. I think that he was afraid to learn, that he had assisted in sending an innocent man to the gallows, just for revenge for something, that might not even be true. The case was as far as I know never mentioned in the Isbell family again, and James has never again paid for any lawyers, neither for the prosecution nor for the defense in any other trials in our county or in any other county.

Besides what Ann Melton told me during our conversation, nobody who was directly connected to the case ever mentioned it after Thomas Dula's execution. None of the Dulas, the Meltons, the Andersons nor any other families closely involved in the matter would ever talk about what happened. This of course made it possible for a lot of different rumors to arise in our neighborhood, and even if I tried to stop some of them, I could not tell what really had happened, so the rumors evolved more and more, and got further away from the truth about what really happened, and they actually still do.

I hope, that in a distant future, when this letter is opened, and nobody remembers the affair, it will somehow create some justice for the people involved, not least Thomas Dula. Should any descendants of Thomas Foster ever read this, I beg your forgiveness for telling the truth of what really happened on that unfortunate Friday in May 1866.

I sincerely believe that what Ann Melton told me was the truth, and my medical experience makes me certain that the death of Laura Foster was an accident and not a premeditated murder. I do not think that anybody would kill another person deliberately with just one single stab to the chest, as he could not even be sure the stab would hit the heart.

Kings Creek, October 1887

With due regard
George Nicholas Carter, MD

Publisher's Epilogue

Before I decided to publish the manuscript, I did a bit of research using the internet, the state archives here in Raleigh and also some of the many book written about the case. I also involved my uncle Michael, who is a minister in a small congregation in the Blue Ridge Mountains, but more important he is the family genealogist and knows a lot about genealogy and where to look for information. From these sources I learned that most of what the doctor wrote in the manuscript was definitely true and could be verified from official records like for instance census records, marriage licenses and so on.

Laura Foster was murdered in May of 1866 and Thomas C. Dula was charged with the murder. The trial started in Wilkesboro but was soon transferred to Statesville and so were Thomas Dula and Ann Melton, who had been accused of taking part in the crime. When Tom was convicted but before his execution, Ann Melton was transferred back to Wilkesboro, where she was acquitted in the fall term of 1868 after which she returned to her husband. I have not been able to determine how she actually died, but I have no reason to distrust Doctor Carter in this, especially as a lot of unconfirmed rumors tell the same story.

Tom actually had three older sisters, that were all married before 1850 and one older sister, Eliza, who never married. He had two older brothers who never returned from the Civil War though I have not been able to determine exactly how they died, but more died from different diseases than from acts of war, so probably they did too. A few years after the execution of Thomas Dula, his mother sold her land and moved in with her oldest daughter, Anna Evangeline who had married one Micajah Hendrix sometime between 1840 and 1850, and Mary Dula lived in her son-in-law's household with Eliza as late as in 1880. This is the last census record that mentions her, while Eliza is mentioned in 1900 as well, now living alone and Anna and Micajah is not mentioned, so they had probably passed away, leaving Eliza to take care of herself.

Tom Dooley was imprisoned together with James Melton and others from the same area in Camp Hammond on Point Lookout in Maryland (one of the worst Union POW camps) in March 1865 and was released in June 1865. He was through his grandfather, Bennett Dula, related to both Juliet Carter and Sarah Louise Isbell as well as to many other people in the area like the doctor wrote, including the witness Pauline Foster, who was his first cousin once removed. Her father appears to have been an illegitimate son of Tom Dooley's uncle, John Dula, known as Jack as Dr. Carter wrote in his manuscript. The mother of this Levi Foster apparently was a daughter of one Robert Foster, an uncle of Laura Foster's father.

Dr. Carter himself was, as I mentioned in one of my previous notes, a second cousin of General Robert E. Lee as his father was a cousin of the general's mother. He did marry Juliet Jones, on her mother's side a second cousin of Tom Dooley, in 1852 and they had three children, a son and two daughters of which one, Julia, died when she was only seven months old and Julia is buried on the Dula-Horton Cemetery in Caldwell County like the doctor wrote. This cemetery was founded by Captain William Dula and today is on the National Register of Historic Places. The doctor and his wife are buried about one mile away on the Mariah's Chapel Methodist Cemetery, where also his son George Hill Carter, who gave my great-great-grandfather the envelope, is buried along with his wife.

One Pinkney Foster served along with James Melton in the 26th North Carolina Infantry and both were wounded at Gettysburg, so I suppose that this was Ann Melton's brother.

Eliza Anderson did have a son with James Isbell and another with Rufus Dula Horton. I have not been able to confirm that Rufus Horton was also the father of her daughter, but I see no reason to doubt the doctor in this. Eliza Anderson never got married, not to Rufus Horton, not to anyone. At the trial she was accused of having a relationship with a man of color, one John Anderson, but she denied this allegation, and I have found no proof of such a relationship.

The Calvin Cowles that the doctor mentioned, did marry his own stepsister, Temperance Martha Duval in 1844 and after her death in 1866, in July 1868 he married Ida Holden, daughter of the then newly elected governor, William Holden. Calvin passed away in 1907 as one of the richest men in North Carolina, while his second wife passed away in 1937 in the ripe age of 91. Thank you, uncle Michael for your insight and help in these matters.

Somewhere in the letter, Dr. Carter wonders why people in the area believed that no jury in North Carolina would convict and hang a white woman, and he refers to one Frankie Silver that everybody knew about, but doesn't elaborate further on this. Frances Steward Silver, known as Frankie, was a young woman, who was convicted of killing her husband in what was then Burke County in 1831, a little over 35 years before the case against Ann Melton went to trial. Frankie Silver was a white woman, and she was found guilty in the murder and in 1833, only 17 years old, she was hanged in Morganton. Probably the story, which actually generated a song, "The Ballad of Frankie Silver" was so well-known that the doctor saw no reason to explain it further. Contrary to the Tom Dooley case of which numerous books have been written, not very much has been written about Frankie Silver. All I was able to find were som articles on the internet, and one book, *"The untold story of Frankie Silver"* by one Percy Young, but at least it told me, what the doctor was referring to.

I could go on like this, but I think this will be enough to prove that most of what the good doctor wrote, can be confirmed, so I have no reason to doubt the things that cannot, like the conversations he had with James Isbell and especially with Ann Melton. I see no reason for him to make up such a story. I believe him, but will leave it up to you to make up your own mind. Did Tom Dooley kill Laura Foster or was an innocent man hanged for a crime he didn't commit, maybe to protect a married woman that he had loved since childhood? A woman who he thought was the guilty party, but who had nothing to do with the murder either, and was only trying to pro- tect her mother, brother and sister?

And finally an evaluation of the case itself that I write as a criminal lawyer of the twenty-first century. I know that things were very different then. It was during the reconstruction period, and the law was handled differently from today. Even if Dr. Carter's story is not correct, which I think it is, Tom Dooley should never have been put to trial at all. After having read what- ever is left of the trial records, I can only come to one conclusion, and that is that the circumstantial evidence was far from strong enough to even arrest Tom Dooley, not to say convict him of murder. Apparently no-one else was ever suspected or at least not looked into, but several people had the opportunity and the means, and probably a motive as well. And the motive that the prosecution claimed that Tom Dooley had to commit the murder was weak to say the least. So yes, Tom Dooley should have been acquitted or better, not arrested,charged by the Grand Jury at all. Hope- fully now his soul can be set free if not his body. And contrary to what I have read in many of the books that I have read about the case, as a crim- inal defense lawyer, I don't think that Zebulon Vance did such a great job; he could have done much more. Maybe he felt the same way himself, which could be the reason why he never mentioned the case in any of his writings, and why his partner in the Charlotte law firm, Clement Dowd, didn't even mention this very spectacular and very public case with a single word in his 1897 biography, *Life of Zebulon B. Vance*.

Raleigh, North Carolina, August 2018

Matthew Murphy, J.D.

A final word from the author

If you have gotten this far, and have gotten interested in this case, and want to know more facts about the case or read more fiction, as I had "Mr. Murphy" tell, several books are written about the case, both facts and fiction.

The first book I ever read was *"The Ballad of Tom Dula"* by John Foster West, written back in 1970. FosterWest was as far as I know the first to actually read the case files, or whatever is left of them, and base his book on these facts. He also used the article from New York Herald that "Dr. Carter" mentions in this novella. Unfortunately, Foster believed a little too much in what this article told about the area around Elkville. But the book is worth reading anyway and it also has transcripts of a lot of the case files that are found in the North Carolina Archives in Raleigh (and now also on the internet).

If you want to know mere about the story and how thorough research can be done, I will recommend what is the most recent book about the case. This book from 2016 is written by Charlotte Corbin Barnes and is called *"The Tom Dooley Files – My Search For The Truth Behind The Legend"*. In this book you not only learn about the case, but also get the story of how Mrs. Barnes conducted her research over a period of 30 years. This is my favorite book about the subject, even if I had read several others. Mrs. Barnes has interviewed several decendants of people involved in the case in order to get their versions of the story. "Meeting" these people, is one of the things that makes this book special, but of course also the way Mrs. Barnes tells the story.

If you like to read more fiction, I will recommend a novel by author and actor Karen Wheeeling Reynolds, *"Tom Dooley – The Story Behind The Ballad"* from 2011. Mrs. Reynolds grew up in the area around Elkville and wrote her novel to keep the legends alive. The solution to the riddle in the novel is very different from the solution, in my novella, and the novel also has a bit more action and a larger cast.

Should you happen to be in Wilkes County in the summertime, you can watch a play, also written by Mrs. Reynolds, that has been performed each summer since 2001 in (or rather at an outdoor theater outside) Wilkesboro. This play, *"Tom Dooley – A Wilkes County Legend"*, is definitely worth seeing, if you are interested in the story and the legends.

In Wilkesboro you can visit the old jail and see the cell where Tom Dooley was incarcerated for a few months in 1866. Also a few artifacts are on display here. The small open-air museum, Whippoorwill Academy and Village in Ferguson in Wilkes County has a selection of paitings and drawings by Edith Ferguson Carter retelling the legend and also a collection of artifacts related to the case. Another interesting collection of records, movie posters and other stuff related to Tom Dooley can be found at Statesville Historical Collection in Statesville, Iredell County, the town where Tom Dooley was hanged.

So if I got you interested in the case, there is a lot for you to read and to do, if you want to know or see more.

Jan Kronsell

Jan Kronsell lives in Denmark, in Brøndby, a Copenhagen suburb.

He has worked as an officer in the Royal Danish Navy, an IBM Systems Engineer and is currently a Business College Teacher.

He has visited Western North Carolina numerous times and has been researching the Tom Dooley case since 2000.

He is the author of Land of Friendliness and Beauty – a Danes Guide to Western North Carolina.